This book is dedicated to my favorite teacher Ms. Davis
-Truman

A Little Tiger Tale

The indicia featured in this book are registered trademarks of the University of Missouri.

A special thanks to Jeff Davis.

For more information, please contact:
Mascot Books
560 Herndon Parkway #120
Herndon, VA 20170
info@mascotbooks.com

CPSIA Code: PRT0816A
ISBN: 978-1-63177-338-9

Printed in the United States

www.mascotbooks.com

A LITTLE TIGER TALE

by Steven Kveton

Illustrated by Carolyn Figuereo

When I was a little kid, I was very shy and did not want to go to school until I met Ms. Davis. She was the best teacher ever!

Every day we played games and sang songs that helped us learn how to read and count.

One day she said, "If you take care of yourself and work hard, you can grow up to be almost anything you want to be but you must do these four things with DETERMINATION."

"But Ms. Davis," I said, "there are so many things I want to be. How do I decide?"

She smiled and said, "Not knowing what to do is the fun part of growing up because you get to try so many different things. I became a teacher because I like helping children learn. What are you good at Truman and what makes you happy?"

Well that's easy, I thought. I will go to college and become the greatest football player for my favorite team: the Missouri Tigers!

Folks, can you believe it? Truman makes another Tiger-iffic catch!

Oh my, look at the little guy go! Truman runs for a touchdown!

Truman throws a long pass then kicks a field goal and wins the game for MIZZOU!

I'm good at picking teams on the playground.
I would be a great coach.

Come on boys, tie your shoelaces and put
on your helmets. Let's show 'em how we play
MIZZOU football!

I like to sing in class. Maybe I'll study music and sing the National Anthem before games.

Or I could learn how to play the tuba and join MARCHING MIZZOU!

Gee, it sure would be cool to sit way up high and be a television announcer.

Wow! What a great first half! The TIGERS scored two touchdowns and a field goal and you had two hotdogs, nachos, fries, and a soda pop.

Wait a minute! I always beat my dad when we play h-o-r-s-e. I'll star for the Missouri basketball team.

And sometimes I hit the ball over the fence at home. I'll just need to practice my catching and throwing.

Or I could be the trainer and help injured players.

Yes, I really do like helping people.

Maybe I will be become a famous doctor or a nurse.

Ms. Davis says I'm good at writing out my alphabet. I could be a reporter for the college newspaper. *"What is your favorite color?"*

I'm good with numbers too. Maybe I'll become a professor.

1 2 3 4 5 6 7 8 9 10

1 2 3 4 5 6 7 8 9 10

$$\frac{+1}{2} \quad \frac{+1}{3} \quad \frac{+1}{4} \quad \frac{+1}{5} \quad \frac{+1}{6} \quad \frac{+1}{7} \quad \frac{+1}{8} \quad \frac{+1}{9} \quad \frac{+1}{10} \quad \frac{+1}{11}$$

MIZ + ZOU = MIZZOU

There are so many things I want to do at MIZZOU!

Then guess what happened to me when I grew up.
With DETERMINATION, I ate right, exercised every day,
and worked hard just like Ms. Davis said.

And I found the job that was just right for me:
being the Missouri Tiger's mascot!

And the best part of my job is
I get to meet nice people like...

YOU

(Insert photo)

TOM
St. Joseph, MO

EMMA
Mexico, MO

JACK
Hannibal, MO

MOLLY
Kansas City, MO

TRUMAN
Columbia, MO

MARTHA
St. Louis, MO

DARREN
Joplin, MO

BEN
Jefferson City, MO

MARIA
Jackson, MO

Many years ago, the people of Boone County, Missouri had a dream: to offer the citizens of our state the promise of a better life through education. In 1839, their dream was realized when 900 people pledged $117,921 and land to establish the first university west of the Mississippi River in Columbia, Missouri. Today the University of Missouri System has grown into one of our country's largest centers for higher education with more than 77,000 students on four campuses and Extension programs throughout the state.

In this book, Ms. Davis encouraged young Truman to enjoy being a child 'because you get to try to do so many different things' while you are growing up. With over 300 degree programs, 20 top tier sports programs, research facilities around the state, and numerous employment opportunities, The University of Missouri continues to offer a world of possibilities to all people.

Truman says…

"If we all work hard with DETERMINATION like the pioneers of Boone County, together we can make the world a better place for everyone!"

UMKC™

™

UMSL™

™

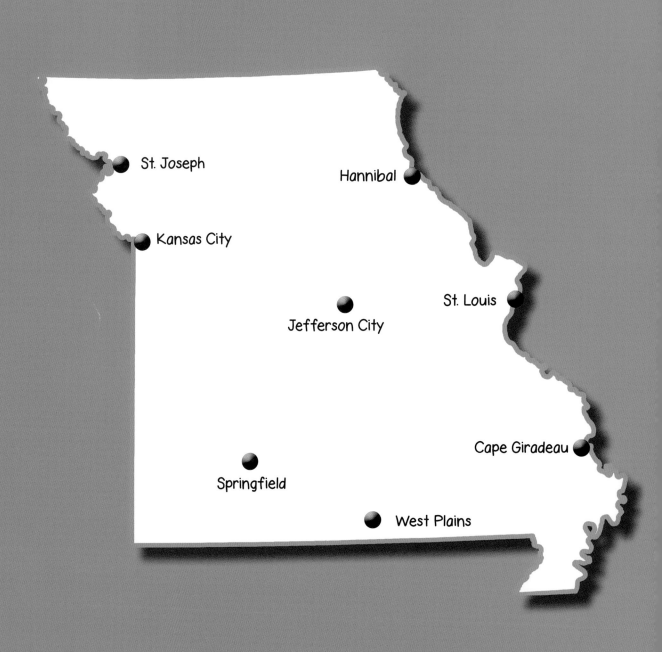

St. Joseph

Hannibal

Kansas City

St. Louis

Jefferson City

Cape Giradeau

Springfield

West Plains

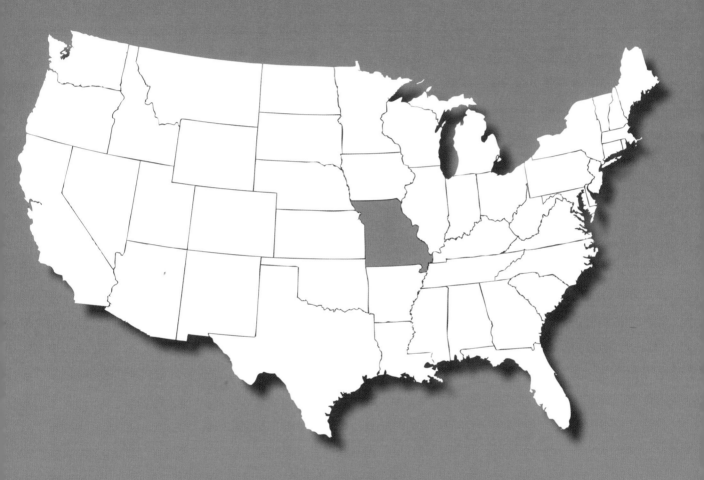

Where do you live?